THE MAGIC ROCK

AN ADVENTURE BY THE SEA

By
Angela Donnelly

MAPLE
PUBLISHERS

The Magic Rock – An Adventure by The Sea

Author: Angela Donnelly

First Published in 2024

ISBN 978-1-83538-236-3 (Paperback)
    978-1-83538-237-0 (Hardback)
    978-1-83538-238-7 (E-Book)

Illustrations by Tony Paultyn

Book Cover Design and Book Layout by:
    White Magic Studios
    www.whitemagicstudios.co.uk

Published by:
    Maple Publishers
    Fairbourne Drive, Atterbury,
    Milton Keynes,
    MK10 9RG, UK
    www.maplepublishers.com

A CIP catalogue record for this title is available from the British Library.

For my boys - My husband and my wonderful children - We did it!

Together we made my dream come true...

&

To Peter & Patricia

For always believing in me.

INDEX

CHAPTER 1

AALIYAH, LIAM, HUDSON & MATTHEW

"Aaliyah!" Liam called to his little sister, as she ran down to the sea edge. "Aaliyah, wait for me!" he shouted but Aaliyah couldn't hear him, she was far too busy playing in the summer sea waves, enjoying the feeling of the water splashing over her dainty toes. She laughed happily as she hopped over a wave that broke in a small crest by her feet. She loved playing in the shallow water.

Aaliyah pushed her long ringlet curls out of her face and spotted Liam running towards her. "Come on Liam!" she called to him.

Aaliyah was only seven years old but she was very mature for her age, probably because she was the youngest of four children and had three older brothers. She had grown up fast and strong.

Liam was the closest to Aaliyah in age at eight years old, he wasn't much taller than her, with dark brown hair and a kind, handsome face. They were the best of friends and they did nearly everything together. Liam was very easy-going and always kind to Aaliyah and she loved him for it.

Aaliyah's brother Hudson was 10 and had the same dark brown hair and a cheerful smiling face, but he was the most mischievous of them all and he loved messy play. He was always covered in dirt, paint or smothering himself in sand, which is where he was at the moment, laying on the beach with Matthew helping to completely cover him in the lovely golden sand so that all you could see was his head!

Matthew was the eldest, tall and slim and at 12 years old he liked to think that he was very grown up - and he could be a little bossy. Aaliyah didn't mind, Matthew was mostly full of fun and only bossy when he felt that he needed to be, so usually Aaliyah would listen to him... but not always, she thought to herself, smirking.

It was the start of the summer holidays and Aaliyah was feeling very contented, Mum and Dad were away with work, so she and her brothers were staying at Nanny's for a full week! Aaliyah had been counting down the days. Nanny's house was the best place in the whole world, it was a cottage by the sea which meant an entire week of playing on the beach and lots of Nanny's lovely baking. Nanny made the best scones and homemade bread that Aaliyah had ever tasted.

"Aaliyah, why didn't you wait for me?" Liam asked, running up, slightly out of breath.

"Sorry, but you were taking so long to get your swim shorts on! I just wanted to get in the sea. I did wait for you, sort of, I've only put my toes in, let's jump in together, shall we?" Aaliyah said smiling sweetly at Liam. "Ok, first one under," Liam replied to his pretty dark-haired sister as he rushed forward into the cooling waves.

Aaliyah hurried to keep up with him and the two of them waded out into the water. They stood together to count down, "3, 2, 1" and with a deep breath, they dived under the wave that was about to break over them. The rush of diving under the water filled Aaliyah with pleasure and as she came back up to the surface, she took a gasp of the fresh air. The feeling of the warm sun on their shoulders as they surfaced was delightful and both Aaliyah and Liam felt like they could do this forever.

"I wish I was a fish," said Liam as he splashed around in the waves.

"I think you already are one!" laughed Aaliyah. She admired the way Liam effortlessly dipped in and out of the water. All four of the children were great swimmers having spent most of their holidays at Nanny's cottage by the sea.

"Yeah, but could you imagine actually being a fish and swimming around all day?" "Wouldn't that be amazing?" Liam joked.

"Bob, bob, bob" was Aaliyah's reply as she pretended to be a fish swimming around in the water.

"Aaliyah, Liam, Matthew, Hudson!" Aaliyah heard Nanny call from far up the beach, "Come on gang, the picnic is ready."

"Oooh yummy," Liam shouted and rushed to the sea edge, "Come on I'm starving!"

Aaliyah smiled as she watched her brothers race for the picnic, shaking her head slightly, thinking about how much they loved their food! Aaliyah was more of a picky eater, but her brothers really enjoyed a good feast, especially Nanny's delicious food.

Aaliyah made her way to the picnic blanket and sat down as Nanny wrapped a towel around her.

"How was the sea?" Nanny asked.

"Awesome!" Liam replied laying back on the blanket, a sandwich already in his hand. They all enjoyed a picnic of ham sandwiches made with Nanny's delicious homemade bread and Liam's favourite, sweet fresh strawberries for dessert. Aaliyah had finished long before the boys and asked, "Can I go back in the water please Nanny?"

"Yes, ok but don't go in too deep until the boys are with you," Nanny warned.

"Ok Nanny," Aaliyah yelled, already halfway down the beach.

Aaliyah stood happily on the shoreline smiling out at the water, she was feeling so contented that it was only day one of her holiday. It was the best feeling, especially with the sun shining down on her and the water splashing around her feet and knowing that there were lots of days like this ahead.

As she stared into the water watching the ebb and flow of the tide push itself up over the warm sand, then pull back into a small wave and then whoosh back up the beach again she noticed something unusual in the water. Something shiny, that appeared to be almost glowing!

The object was only a few steps away from her, bright and glimmering in the shallow water and it seemed to be beckoning her to come closer, almost like a magnet pulling her towards it.

She began to wade out towards it, stepping very carefully, she was afraid that if she moved too fast it might dislodge and disappear into the waves before she could get to it.

The water felt cold against her legs, her warm feet needed to readjust to the cool sea temperature, but Aaliyah barely noticed. She just kept moving forward until the shiny shimmering object was right in front of her.

What on earth is it? She thought, peering down at it. It appeared to be a strange shaped rock that was practically glowing, it shimmered and shone sending out rays of colourful light through the water. It was very unusual!

When she first looked at it, it seemed to be a very large rock but then on her next glance it appeared really small. It was almost like it was growing and shrinking before her eyes. It was not like any rock that she had ever seen before. Small and beautiful but also big and glowing at the same time. She was completely mesmerised by it! It was so captivating she felt like she couldn't look away.

Aaliyah knelt down in the shallow water, her eyes still glued to the rock. Very carefully and slowly she reached out in front of her. She had such a strong urge to touch it. She leaned forward a little more and as her hand touched the rock, in an instant, everything changed!

Aaliyah felt dizzy as though she was travelling on a super-fast roller coaster ride and before she knew what was happening, she was under the water, completely submerged, as if the tide had risen up and covered her! The water was ebbing and flowing, dragging her forward and back. She could feel herself being pulled by the current…. she was being dragged far away from the rock…. she was being taken out to sea!

Help me! What's happening? Aaliyah was really frightened now! She did not want to be dragged any further out to sea and the current was rolling her around and around as though she was trapped in a whirlpool.

She tried to stand but standing didn't work, it was as if her legs had disappeared, no pain or discomfort just not there anymore. Her legs were missing! The thought was terrifying and Aaliyah began to panic!

She tried to pull herself forward with her arms, but her arms did not feel normal either! It didn't feel like they were missing but they felt really strange. She couldn't pull them forward, all she could do was twist them around and around. Flapping pointlessly.

She tried and tried to swim or stand, but all she could do was flap helplessly about, lost in the water! Aaliyah experimented with wiggling her bottom from side to side and that seemed to help, she could balance much better now! Next, she tried combining the wiggle where her legs should be with a flap of her strange arms and success - she shot forward in the water! She was swimming! Around and around she went, practising the movement.

After a little while it started to feel really easy, using the technique of wiggling her bottom while flapping her strange arms forward and back, Aaliyah found that she could move around in the water with ease and speed. She could even twist and turn in the water, she felt great!

For just a few seconds Aaliyah was actually enjoying herself until the realisation that she was still in danger flashed through her thoughts. She was still stuck under the water!

*Oh my gosh… I **must** need some air…, I **must** need to breathe, her mind started racing.*

Up! I have to go up, towards the sunlight.

Aaliyah forced herself not to panic but to continue to wiggle and flap, wiggle and flap and it worked, she pulled herself easily towards the surface of the water. She could see the sun high in the sky, it looked warm and welcoming. She hurried to burst into the fresh air but as she got above the water and opened her mouth to take a deep breath, something felt very wrong! It was as if she couldn't pull the air into her body, like she was suffocating in the warm sea breeze.

Aaliyah quickly dropped back down below the surface again and now she was really afraid.

She needed to breathe; how long could she survive underwater without oxygen?

The current was still trying to drag her out to sea, although her wiggle and flap motion was easily strong enough to hold her in place, but she desperately wanted to breathe. She needed to take a deep gasp of air even though she was stuck underwater.

Aaliyah's survival instincts were taking over and the need to fill her lungs with oxygen was overwhelming. She was panicking, trying her hardest to hold her breath for as long as she could. She didn't want to drown! But it was no use, she knew that breathing was involuntary, it just happens, she could feel her mouth opening and sucking in the water and –

oh my goodness it was the strangest thing, it felt fine!

With her mouth open or closed she was breathing in the water and somehow, she was getting enough oxygen! Aaliyah was filled with pure elation. I can breathe! She thought and she celebrated by twisting and turning around and around in the water.

As she started to calm down, she took a moment to concentrate on just her breathing, I don't know how I'm doing this but I'm ok! she thought to herself, feeling very relieved.

For a few seconds, she felt really good, swimming and breathing happily in the sea but the reality of her situation soon dawned on her, she was still in terrible danger. How was she going to get back to normal? She was trapped under the water and she couldn't stand up!

She tried her hardest to look down at herself to see if she could figure out what was happening with her legs, but she just kept going around in circles, around and around she went as she attempted to bend to see her own body. This really is so strange! She thought.

Aaliyah floated in place, for a little while, breathing but not sure how and trying hard to assess her situation. 'I can't find my legs, but I can wiggle my bottom! I can feel my arms, but I can't pull them in front of my face! What has happened to me? This really is so bizarre! And what am I going to do now? How do I get back to normal?' She questioned herself.

I just want to be back on the beach with Nanny! And that's when the thought occurred to her, of course! My brothers and Nanny. They will notice that I'm not at the sea edge anymore. Nanny will be worried, they will definitely come looking for me! Aaliyah reassured herself, Ok Aaliyah, ok, don't panic! When they notice that you are missing, they will come. The best thing you can do is to be somewhere they can find you!

Aaliyah was a clever girl and it didn't take her long to figure out that if she swam back up to the surface, she could have a good look around and hopefully work out where she was in the ocean.

I will need to hold my breath or hold some water in my mouth before I put my head out of the sea, she decided. It had felt so awful last time, like trying to breathe through a completely blocked snorkel!

This is so weird, she thought as she took a deep gulp of the seawater before cautiously raising her head into the fresh air. She used her strange arms and started to circle around scanning for any sign of Nanny's beach. One direction definitely took her further out to sea with nothing but water and clear blue sky to be seen, so she twisted around fighting the pull of the waves and there, far away in the distance, she could just about make out her family still sitting on the picnic blanket on Nanny's beach, completely unaware of the danger that she was in.

As happy as she was to spot them in the distance, she was very dismayed to see how far away they were. She had been swept a long way from the shore and Aaliyah suddenly realised that her strange little body was feeling really tired. The constant fight against the current was exhausting. She felt so drained and worn out that she wanted to cry. 'I've got so far to swim' she thought as she began to sob, but to her surprise, she found that there were no tears. 'Of course, I can't cry underwater' she said to herself. 'My only hope is to swim all the way back! Ok Aaliyah, come on, you can do it!' she said firmly to herself and down into the water she went setting off in the direction of the beach.

It was quite a surprise to Aaliyah that it didn't take her very long at all. She swam with such ease through the water that she even started to enjoy it. 'This is amazing!' Aaliyah admitted to herself. The journey which had seemed so daunting at first really only took her a minute or two. It was as if she had magic swimming powers, the speed she swam was incredible, flipping through the water, wiggle and flap, wiggle and flap and by the time she reached the shoreline she was delighted with this new and wonderful feeling. The freedom, the speed and the power that her little body had as it went whizzing through the water was quite unbelievable.

She slowed as she came close to the shore and wondered what to do next. 'Should I just keep splashing about?' She questioned. 'Surely someone will notice me if I just keep splashing!' Aaliyah thrashed around making as much of a commotion as she possibly could, until she became aware that she was completely hidden by the waves. She realised in that moment that the sea was always going to out-splash her!

'What am I going to do now?' Aaliyah was trying not to panic.

Then suddenly, from the corner of her eye, Aaliyah noticed something bright and glowing shining in the water. The rock, the glimmering beautiful rock, it was still there, giving off its colourful glow!

'The rock! I wonder if I touch it, will I return to normal?' Aaliyah thought excitedly to herself. With a glimmer of hope, she swam in its direction. She reached the rock in no time at all, swimming felt like second nature to her now. It was easy, she could dart around in any direction. Like the breathing, she had got used to it surprisingly quickly.

As she reached the rock she stopped and pondered for a moment. 'Now what do I do?' Touching the rock was the last thing that she remembered before everything had changed. 'I guess I have to touch it again,' she thought.

She swam around and around darting here and there and gathering up her courage. 'What if it makes things worse? What if I disappear altogether?' she thought. 'I suppose it can't get much worse, can it?' she reasoned with herself, 'and I can't stay like this forever!' Forcing herself to be brave she moved cautiously forward attempting to touch the rock with what she assumed was still her nose. She nuzzled into it and !BOP! she did it, she touched the rock!

Nothing happened!!

"Oh no nothing happened," she gasped feeling incredibly disappointed.

"What now?"

'Maybe I should touch it with my hand?' It was my hand that touched it last time so maybe that was how to get it to work.

Aaliyah worked hard using her new swimming skills to adjust herself so that she was parallel to the rock. The swell of the sea and the motion of the waves were pulling her in different directions, but she finally managed to get beside the rock and flapping her strange feeling hands she did it, she touched the rock! !BOP!

Nothing! No change!

An overwhelming feeling of fatigue and exhaustion came over Aaliyah. She wanted to cry but there were no tears in the sea, so she just floated, feeling like she was crying but not able to tell if there were even any actual tears flowing into the saltwater surrounding her.

What am I going to do? She sobbed pointlessly, feeling very alone in the water.

And that's when it came to her - her final hope, I need my family, my Nanny, Matthew, Hudson and Liam. They will help me, I know they will.

Aaliyah deeply regretted racing down to the shore without Liam. Liam was always by her side. He was her best friend. Oh, how she wished Liam was beside her now.

"Liam," she called with all her might. "Liam, please come and help me!" She screamed as loudly as she could. "Liam!" she hollered over and over again and with every scream a lively stream of bubbles popped from her mouth. "LIAM!!!"

⊷⊶⊰◈⊱⊷⊶

CHAPTER 2

LIAM TO THE RESCUE

Liam was lying contentedly on the picnic blanket beside Nanny. He was staring up at the sky watching a single light fluffy cloud move slowly away into the distance. He had eaten lots of delicious sandwiches and was relaxing with a half-eaten juicy strawberry in his hand. His brothers had already run off to the rock pools and were busy digging a trench from one rock pool to another, allowing the flow of water from the large pool to drain into the smaller pool.

'This is the best day ever!' he thought, smiling to himself.

Nanny was busy packing the remainder of the picnic into the little basket, collecting any bits of rubbish and gathering everything together. "Liam," Nanny said. "Could you pass me that water bottle please?" "Of course," Liam replied and rolled over onto his stomach to grab the empty water bottle for Nanny.

Liam was enjoying the peaceful, calm day. There was hardly any noise apart from the rustling of Nanny clearing up, the background splash of the waves and the shrill call of seagulls. Further along the beach his brothers were laughing and chatting while they worked on their trench "Look, look, it's working!" he could hear Matthew shouting. Liam smiled as he watched a small stream of water run along the tunnel his brothers had made.

Suddenly Liam noticed another noise, a strange noise, an unusual sound like bubbles popping in the distance.

Liam raised himself to his knees and looked around curiously. "What was that?" he said to Nanny. "What was what darling?" Nanny replied distracted with fitting everything into the basket. Liam paused and listened carefully, but he couldn't hear anything anymore. "Nothing," Liam said "It's okay." And he lay back down.

Pop, pop, pop, pop, there it was again. Liam was certain that he could hear something this time. He got himself back up onto his knees and dropped the stalk of the strawberry into Nanny's rubbish bag. "All done," he said "Thank you Nanny" and he started off down the beach.

The popping noise seemed to get louder as he got closer to the water, so he continued to follow it along the shoreline. Pop, pop, pop, it was like strange sounding bubbles bursting in the water.

As he walked along the beach trying to identify the source of the unusual noise, he realised that he couldn't see Aaliyah.

"Aaliyah where are you?" he called out.

There was no reply.

That's strange, he thought, she only ran down here a little while ago. "Aaliyah," he called again. Still no reply. 'Where has she gone?' he wondered, splashing through the shallow water.

Below the water, Aaliyah could see Liam.

"Liam, I'm here!" she shouted causing an avalanche of bubbles to pop around her. Liam was standing just a few steps away from her. Aaliyah swam towards him and started splashing about desperately, hoping to catch his attention. But he did not look down. "Please look down Liam. Please help me," Aaliyah begged willing her brother to see her...

"Oh I wish I was standing beside Liam, Oh I wish I was standing beside Liam, Oh I wish I was standing beside Liam," Aaliyah repeated desperately. Every part of her body was pleading for her wish to come true and then suddenly !**POOF**! With a slight whoosh of her body like a ride on a fast rollercoaster, Aaliyah opened her eyes and - she was on the beach!

She was completely back to her normal self, sitting in the shallow water. Aaliyah sat for a moment wiggling her toes and kicking her legs feeling very relieved when she suddenly realised that poor Liam was standing right beside her looking utterly shocked. Her sudden reappearance had given him quite a fright.

"Oh Liam you saved me!" Aaliyah sobbed, throwing her arms around his neck.

Liam looked scared stiff. "What just happened? You appeared out of nowhere!" Liam yelled. "Aaliyah you really scared me!" he continued to scold her. "That was not funny! And where did you come from?"

Aaliyah paid no attention, planting kisses on his cheek and saying, "Thank you Liam," she ran as fast as her legs could carry her up the beach throwing herself into her Nanny's arms.

Nanny was about to tell Aaliyah off as the girl almost knocked her off her feet, but then she noticed Aaliyah's face and saw the fear and the relief of a frightened little girl staring up at her so, instead, she pulled Aaliyah into a tight squish hug. Nanny waited until Aaliyah had relaxed a little before asking "Are you ok? what's wrong?"

Aaliyah didn't know where to start, "I was down the beach," she began, sobbing a little into Nanny's jumper. "I was standing in the sea and I saw something in the water and I touched it and then..." but to Aaliyah's surprise, she couldn't finish her sentence. Her voice suddenly changed and all that came out of her mouth was "blob, gulp, glop, glwp..." The more Aaliyah tried to explain the more strange noises came from her mouth. No words, just the strangest sounds!

"Aaliyah it's ok darling, calm down, you are not making any sense," Nanny said calmly.

"In the sea Nanny, there was something in the sea!"

Nanny looked at Aaliyah and the biggest most beaming smile that Aaliyah had ever seen spread across her face, her eyes were lit up and sparkling. Aaliyah had never seen Nanny look so happy, Nanny was practically glowing.

"Oh Aaliyah," she said and pulled her into another tight, tight hug. "It's ok darling, don't worry, I've got you. Just stay by me for a little bit," she reassured her.

"Boys!" Nanny called out, hardly able to contain her excitement. "We won't stay much longer, I'd like to go back to the cottage soon, I've got a story to tell you all..."

CHAPTER 3

THE SLEEP OVER

After gathering the remaining bits left on the beach and with one more shout to the boys that it was time to go, they started on their short walk back to the cottage.

The cottage was high up on a cliff that overlooked the beautiful beach where Aaliyah and her brothers had been playing. Aaliyah loved everything about Nanny's home, it was perfect. It was small but so pretty with clean white walls, dark brown window frames and a little metal gate that had a bell attached that tinkled every time the gate was opened.

'Nanny's cottage is magical' Aaliyah thought, smiling to herself, she was already feeling safer as they got closer to Nanny's home. It was a short, steep walk up the cliff to Nanny's cottage but by the time Aaliyah had trudged up the sheer path she was beginning to feel a lot better. The terrifying sensation of being stuck under the water was starting to feel like an unbelievable dream.

Nanny's cottage only had two little bedrooms, one was an actual bedroom for Nanny and the other room was kitted out as Nanny's sewing room. Aaliyah loved the sewing room. It was a den packed full of treasures. It had everything crafty that you could possibly imagine from sewing machines and overlockers to beads, crochet hooks, knitting needles, pens, paper, paints and wool. There were boxes of material everywhere and Aaliyah would often spend hours in there, with Nanny, making decorative cushions or creating teddies and toys from pieces of fabric. But Aaliyah wasn't interested in the sewing room tonight, she was feeling tired and very impatient to hear Nanny's story.

"Tell us your story please Nanny," she begged.

"Not yet sweetheart," Nanny replied gently. "Let me get you all fed and settled in first."

"Actually Aaliyah, can you and the boys make up the beds please?"

"Yes sure," Aaliyah replied with an impatient sigh. "Come on boys," she called to her brothers.

Making up the beds was always fun. Because the cottage only had two small bedrooms, whenever Aaliyah and her brothers came to stay, Nanny would pull down a supply of small mattresses from her large attic that ran the whole length of the bungalow. The attic was where Nanny stored all her large items and with the mattresses made up into comfortable little beds the four of them would cuddle up together on the lounge floor, each child on their mattress with a sleeping bag and a pillow. It was like having a proper campout in Nanny's lounge! It was brilliant and all the children loved it.

Aaliyah and her brothers quickly and happily set about moving furniture out of the way and put the four single mattresses on the floor, covered them in sheets and placed their pillows and sleeping bags untidily on top of them.

"There," Matthew said "All done Nanny."

Nanny popped her head in the door, "Great, thanks gang, dinner is nearly ready."

"What are we having?" Liam asked looking forward to his dinner as usual.

"I've cooked your favourite, tomato pasta with melted cheese and for good boys and girls I have got ice cream for a treat." She said, smiling at them.

Hudson was thrilled. "Great, thanks Nanny," he said, rubbing his tummy. The salty sea air always made him so hungry.

At the table they all sat quietly, munching away, they had quite an appetite after their busy day on the beach, but all Aaliyah could think about was Nanny's story, what was it? Did she know about the magic rock? And why had she been unable to talk properly when she was trying to tell Nanny all about it? She had so many questions.

After they were all full and had eaten two helpings of ice cream, Nanny agreed to tell her story, so with all four of them cuddled up in their sleeping bags, Nanny sat on a little chair beside them and said. "Ok, how do I begin? I suppose it's not really a story it's more like some information that I want to tell you." 'Gosh, this is difficult to explain' she thought looking at the children's expectant expressions as they waited for her to begin.

"Do you all remember that I have said many times that our beach is magical?" Nanny said.

"Yes," they all nodded. "Well, I wasn't lying! When I was a little girl, my father sat me down and told me the same thing that I am about to tell you. There is something down there, something that you cannot talk about even when you want to, but it is there!" Nanny explained carefully. "When you try to talk about it, the words get sort of muddled up in your mouth. It is part of the magic I suppose and it is a little hard to explain, but there is magic on that beach."

Matthew laughed "Really Nanny?" he sounded doubtful. "Yes," said Nanny, "There is something down there and it's very special. When you touch it, you begin a whole new adventure! You can visit an entirely different world! I'm afraid I can't explain it any clearer, but Aaliyah knows, don't you sweetheart?"

Aaliyah was nodding so enthusiastically that Hudson thought her head was going to fall off. "Yes! Yes! I know Nanny" she said, beaming with excitement.

"What do you mean?" Liam asked. He was listening intently from the comfort of his little made-up bed, but he looked very confused. "I don't understand."

Nanny shook her head in frustration "I mean magic is real, on our beach something unusual happens. It's not always there but when it is..." Nanny drifted off into her memories for a moment with a smile on her face that Aaliyah would never forget. "And what I am trying to tell you is that it's ok," she continued "I am confident that you won't come to any harm. I have been on some adventures and now it's your turn and *you are allowed.*"

The boys looked even more confused. "We are allowed to do what?" Matthew asked.

Aaliyah felt like she was going to burst she had so much that she wanted to ask, "So, you've been where I've been, Nanny?" she carefully worded her first question.

"Yes, darling, I have," Nanny replied and added, "Isn't it wonderful?"

Aaliyah wasn't completely sure if it was wonderful. It had felt very scary being out in the deep water all alone. "Weren't you scared?" she asked.

"Well, I was at first," Nanny replied honestly "But once you know the secret of how to return to normal then it's no longer scary, it's just amazing and you four are so lucky to be a part of it."

The boys were looking completely confused. "Nanny, what are you talking about?" Matthew asked, his bewilderment obvious. None of this made any sense to him.

Nanny didn't reply to Matthew's question partly because she couldn't give a clear explanation and partly because Aaliyah had asked a question at the same time and that was the question that needed answering.

"What is the secret to return?" Aaliyah had asked.

The boys looked at Aaliyah wondering what on earth she was talking about. Return from where? Nanny looked directly at Aaliyah and said clearly "Repeat at least three times and wish with all your might!" Nanny turned to the boys and continued "Boys, Aaliyah has got something to show you tomorrow but for tonight I think we should brush our teeth and get some rest. It's going to be a busy day" and with a beaming smile, she got up and headed out of the room.

"Aaliyah what is going on?"

"What happened to you?"

"What's the secret?"

The boys all talked at once.

Aaliyah gave a knowing smile, just like Nanny's and said, "I promise I will show you tomorrow... if I can!" she added hastily. Aaliyah yawned and rubbed her tired eyes, "I agree with Nanny, let's go to sleep and we can get up early." And with that, the boys had to be content until the morning.

The children headed to Nanny's little bathroom and quickly brushed their teeth, all three boys still trying to get answers out of Aaliyah. Liam whispered in her ear, "Aaliyah can you tell me? Just me?" He pleaded. "I wish I could," Aaliyah replied "I just don't know how." Liam looked a little upset, Aaliyah always told him everything why wouldn't she tell him this? With a grumpy face, Liam turned away and started to wash his hands. Aaliyah sighed, she was feeling very frustrated, she wanted more than anything to tell Liam all about what had happened. 'He probably wouldn't believe me anyway' she thought to herself.

A few minutes later all four children were cuddled up in their beds in the middle of Nanny's lounge. Aaliyah had crawled into her cosy sleeping bag and it felt so good, safe and warm. She looked around at her brothers wondering what was going to happen tomorrow. Would the rock still be there? Would she be able to show them?

Nanny came into the room and tucked each of them into their sleeping bags, she kissed them on their foreheads and standing by the door she whispered, "I'm so excited for you all, I've waited so long for this to happen, let the adventures begin!"

But Aaliyah didn't hear Nanny, she was already drifting off to sleep, dreaming of floating in the sea and swimming through the ocean.

CHAPTER 4

IS THE ROCK STILL THERE?

The next morning Aaliyah was snuggled in her warm sleeping bag with her eyes still closed enjoying the comfort of her little bed. She could hear her brothers playing in the garden, "Hudson stop it, it's my turn, give it back" and she could picture Liam chasing Hudson, pulling the ball off him and racing to the other side of Nanny's pretty garden.

Nanny's garden, at the back of the cottage, was full of plants, apple trees, pear trees and cherry trees. There was a small vegetable patch in one corner where Nanny grew herbs and spices and the rest of the garden was a neatly mowed lawn. Aaliyah loved the sweet scent of lavender and mint that filled the air when you went near Nanny's vegetable patch. The front of Nanny's cottage had a smaller patch of grass with a raised rocky wall flower bed that was a joy to climb on because you could stand looking at the view of the cliff that dropped down to the beach below. You could see where the sea and sky met each other. It was a view like no other.

Aaliyah's thoughts drifted sleepily back to the magic rock and how it had felt to swim so freely in the sea and then suddenly she was wide awake. "Oh my gosh, did that really happen? Was it all a dream?" she said out loud. She quickly threw a dressing gown over her shoulders, smiled good morning to Matthew who was half in and half out of his sleeping bag absorbed in some game on his phone and ran into the kitchen where Nanny was busy making some of her delicious scones.

"Nanny, was it real?" She asked excitedly. Nanny smiled and nodded sweetly at Aaliyah. "Let's have some breakfast and head down to the beach shall we?"

"Yes please!" Aaliyah replied her tummy churning with excitement. She did not feel afraid this morning, the fear seemed to be completely swept aside with the excitement and joy of the possibility of exploring this new world. This time Aaliyah was going to be so much braver, she decided. She knew how to return and her brothers would be with her. She was much safer with her big brothers, they had looked after and taken care of her, all her life and if they were beside her then she was confident that everything would be fine.

I hope the rock is still there! I hope my brothers can make the magic work! Aaliyah wished with all her might.

She barely touched the delicious bowl of porridge with sweet syrup dribbled on top. It was usually Aaliyah's favourite breakfast but all she could think about was what if the boys couldn't get it to work? What if it only happened to her? A level of sadness clouded her mind for a moment. It won't be the same if they aren't with me, I don't even think I want to touch the rock again if I am all alone, she decided.

After rushing breakfast Aaliyah hurried her brothers and Nanny out of the door, "Come on, come on, we need to go!" Aaliyah half shouted at everyone, she could hardly contain her excitement and nervousness for the day ahead.

"Oh Matthew, get off your phone, *please!*" Aaliyah said to her brother, "Let's go."

Everyone was finally ready and Aaliyah skipped eagerly ahead of them, full of anticipation. Nanny smiled knowingly and watched Liam hurry along the clifftop to catch up with her, he could feel her energy and he was excited to see what Aaliyah was so desperate to show them.

The short walk to the beach seemed to take forever and Aaliyah had already taken off her shorts and t-shirt and was down to her bathers before Matthew and Hudson had even stepped foot on the sand. "Come on, come on!" She yelled to everyone.

With one last approving smile from Nanny, Aaliyah and Liam bounded down to the shoreline, "Where is it? Where is it?" she muttered, searching the shoreline for any signs of the magic rock's shimmering glow.

"Oh my goodness, Aaliyah, where is what?" An exasperated Liam said, looking all around him but only seeing the rocks at the top of the beach, the soft sand around his feet and the calm sea in front of him. Everything looked just as it always did.

At last, Aaliyah spotted it. It had moved slightly from where it had been the day before, but it was still there, large yet small, glowing and shimmering in the water.

"Wow" said Liam catching a glimpse of what Aaliyah had been frantically searching for and was now pointing at triumphantly. He stood quietly staring at it for a moment. He was quite mesmerised by the beautiful rock.

"That's it, *that's* what I wanted to show you." Aaliyah said her tone hushed as she stood in awe of the glimmering rock.

"It is beautiful," Liam replied "but I don't understand why you are so excited, it is just a rock, it's a stunning rock, but still just a rock!"

"Touch it," Aaliyah said with a huge grin on her face "Go on touch it." Liam stepped forward cautiously dipping his toes in the cool water. "Wait!" Aaliyah grabbed his arm, "I just need to tell you something first!" she thought for a second and choosing her words carefully she said,

"You can breathe!"

"Of course I can breathe," Liam laughed shaking his head at his sister and rolling his eyes. What on earth was she going on about?"

"No I mean, just trust me, don't panic - and breathe. Ok?"

"Ok," Liam said looking seriously confused as he took a small step closer to the rock.

The cool waves were splashing over Liam and Aaliyah's legs as they stood together inches away from the rock, but neither of them really noticed the temperature of the water, the lure of the rock was too strong.

Liam reached down and gently placed his hand on the rock. Aaliyah watched as a colourful glow seemed to cover him and then !**POOF**! Liam was gone! There was just a shimmering glow where Liam had been standing, half a second before.

Aaliyah looked up towards Nanny, Matthew and Hudson and seeing Nanny's reassuring smile Aaliyah touched the rock again... *Whoosh* - Aaliyah felt the familiar feeling of a roller coaster ride and then suddenly she was under the water.

Wiggle and flap, wiggle and flap, the movement was easy to her now but there was no sign of Liam. Aaliyah twisted and turned in the water looking for what she supposed would be a miniature sized Liam splashing around in the water but there was no sign of him. Where had he gone? Had he been dragged out to sea? Aaliyah started to feel frightened again.

'What had she done to Liam? Why had she brought him into this?'

Spinning around and around Aaliyah frantically searched the water, "Where are you Liam?" She yelled and bubbles popped all around her as they exploded out of her mouth.

A short distance ahead of her Aaliyah caught a glimpse of a very tiny fish, it was mainly grey in colour but had the shiniest scales that Aaliyah had ever seen, scales that had a red shimmer giving the whole fish a glowing red aura. The poor fish looked very distressed darting around looking lost and tiny in the swell of the sea. It was being pulled in different directions and was clearly trying to get to the surface.

"Liam?" Aaliyah questioned. He's a fish? Oh my gosh, he's a fish... wait, I'm a fish! The realisation flooded through her like an electric shock. I'm a fish! Aaliyah hurried forward, wiggle and flap, wiggle and flap until she was right in front of the terrified little slither of a fish, "Liam?" She questioned with her mouth open and bubbles popping everywhere. The panicking fish stopped flipping in all directions and looked straight at her.

"Liam if that's you then breathe, just breathe, you won't drown I promise." Aaliyah bubbled at him. She watched as the tiny fish opened its mouth slightly and instantly started calming down. For a short while, Aaliyah floated beside the grey, red-scaled fish, giving the little Liam-fish a chance to compose itself and come to terms with what had just happened. Suddenly something even more surprising happened, if that was even possible, as a cascade of bubbles popped all around her Aaliyah heard the little Liam-fish say "Aaliyah?"

"Liam is that you?" Aaliyah asked with her own bubbles spilling out of her mouth

"Yes," the grey-red fish replied.

"We can talk!! We can talk underwater." Aaliyah's excited sentence sent out thousands more bubbles to dance all around them.

"Aaliyah what is happening?" said a frightened little Liam fish.

"Liam it's ok, this is what happened to me yesterday! This is what Nanny was trying to explain. Touching the magic rock has changed us into, well I guess it's changed us into fish!"

"Oh my gosh, this is amazing!" Liam exclaimed as he started to get into the rhythm of the wiggle and flap motion. Liam shot here and there around Aaliyah and she darted back and forth playing a frantic game of chase under the water. What a feeling!

"Ummm this might be a silly question," Liam bubbled after the two of them had worn themself out swimming around and around "But how do we get back to normal?"

"Oh that's easy," Aaliyah bubbled back. "We just wish with all our might and say it out loud at least three times, watch I'll show you." "I wish I was back to normal, I wish I was back to normal, I wish I was back to normal." And as she wished with every part of her body - !**POOF**! the roller coaster ride feeling again and there she was back in the shallows of the sea.

A few seconds later Liam appeared a short distance away from her. "Oh my gosh, Aaliyah THAT WAS AWESOME! Let's do it again!"

"I think we better fetch Matthew and Hudson" Aaliyah said and Liam nodded enthusiastically, "Yes, let's get them."

CHAPTER 5

MATTHEW AND HUDSON'S TURN

"Nanny, Nanny, it happened again." Aaliyah and Liam yelled running back up the beach to where Nanny had laid the picnic blanket on the sand.

Nanny looked excited as Liam continued "You won't believe what just happened I touched the blob, glwp, gulp, gurgle." Strange noises, no words! 'What's happened to my voice?' Liam looked very confused.

Aaliyah just laughed at Liam's strange sounds, "Do you see what I mean Liam? You can't explain, even when you try."

"Oh I see," Liam said, now he understood Aaliyah's frustration yesterday. Nanny was laughing and beaming at them both, but Hudson and Matthew's confused expressions were comical.

Liam, Aaliyah and Nanny laughed heartily... "Come on, let's show them," Aaliyah said.

"Ok," said Nanny kneeling on the blanket so she could look all four children in the eyes. "But I have got three rules before you go. Number one, Matthew is in charge, he's the oldest and I know he will keep you safe, but you must promise to listen to him!" The three children nodded in agreement while Matthew said proudly, "I will look after them, Nanny."

"Number two," Nanny continued "You must keep checking in with me, I am happy to sit here waiting for you but I need to know that you are safe so please don't be gone for too long."

Again, all four children nodded enthusiastically. "And thirdly and this is my most important rule, I want you to have the time of your lives!" She said beaming lovingly at her beautiful grandchildren, that look of pure love that only an adoring Nanny can give. She hugged them all in turn and said, "Ok gang, off you go" and the four of them headed down to the shoreline.

Running excitedly together across the warm sand, they reached the edge of the water quickly. The sunshine was beaming down on them, it was the start of the most glorious day.

At the sea edge, Aaliyah proudly pointed to the large but small shimmering rock. "That's so cool," Hudson said, staring at it in awe.

"It is very nice," Matthew said "but it's not really *that* exciting," although, weirdly, he couldn't seem to take his eyes off it. "Wait until you touch it." Liam replied, bouncing around with excitement. Aaliyah stood in front of her brothers, enjoying the feeling of being in charge and said confidently "Ok, Liam if you go first then you will already be there when the rest of us... umm arrive!" Aaliyah didn't really know how else to say it, "I will show these two what to do."

"Ok," Liam agreed and he waded straight up to the rock, reached out his hand and smirking at his brothers, touched it and -!**POOF**! Liam disappeared in a colourful glow.

Matthew and Hudson were shocked and stood with their mouths wide open, terrified and amazed at the same time! What just happened?

"Right, Matthew you go next." Aaliyah said happily. "What? No way!" Matthew yelled "Where is he? Where is Liam?" he sounded panicked. Aaliyah laughed "It's ok Matthew, just trust me, ooh and don't forget you can breathe!" "What?" Matthew sounded almost hysterical now.."Just touch the rock," Aaliyah said patiently.

Matthew looked at Aaliyah's reassuring face. He trusted his little sister, she was as sweet as they came and she would never do him any harm, he knew that. Very slowly and very carefully Matthew edged towards the rock. He started reaching out his hand, but then immediately changed his mind. "No, no, no, I don't want to touch it!" he shouted in panic and pulled his hand back.

"Matthew just touch the rock," Aaliyah insisted, a little frustrated with her brother *"Just touch the rock*!" "Ok, ok!" Matthew replied and this time he closed his eyes as he reached out his hand !**POOF**! Just like Liam, Matthew disappeared into a colourful glow.

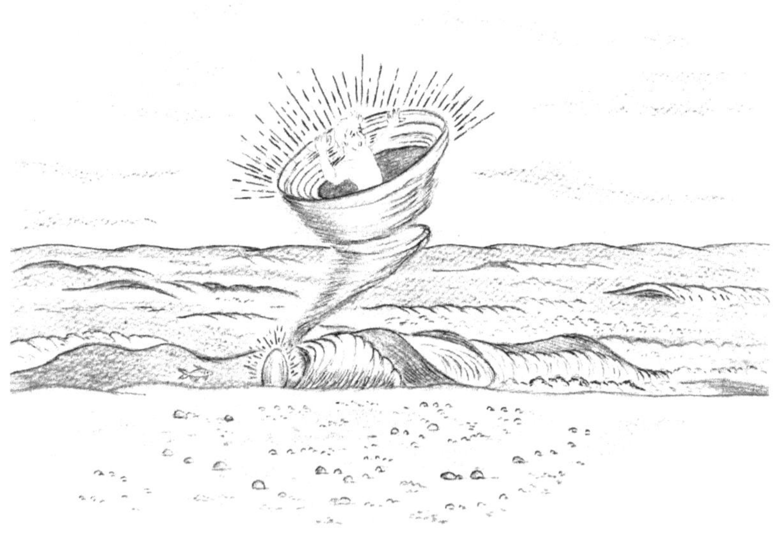

Aaliyah turned her attention to Hudson. "Right, your turn!" she said ignoring his terrified expression. "Do you promise it's safe Aaliyah?"

"Yes! but just remember that you can breathe!"

"Ok," Hudson replied, he was clearly feeling very anxious but he waded bravely forward and reached out his hand to touch the rock. !**POOF**! Hudson was gone.

Aaliyah looked up the beach, gave a friendly wave to Nanny and leant over to touch the rock.

CHAPTER 6

UNDER THE SEA

The familiar feel of the sea surrounding Aaliyah felt wonderful and she giggled to herself as she used her little arms to circle around, searching the water for her brothers. They were easy to find, the three tiny, greyish-coloured fish were making quite a commotion as they splashed and darted about in different directions.

The red-glowing Liam fish was trying to calm his terrified brothers. "Breathe, it's ok, you can breathe" Liam bubbled at them.

The fish all looked identical in size and shape but with one very slight variation, the coloured glow that shone from the scales of each of them was a different colour. Aaliyah had recognised Liam's red glow instantly, especially because he was the calmest of the three fish, but the other two had different colours, a bright green glow and a yellow-orange colour that shone through the water like sunlight.

"Boys, boys, boys," Aaliyah bubbled loudly "What colour am I?"

"What?" The fish with the bright green glow bubbled. Matthew was obviously surprised by the sound of his bubbly voice.

"What colour am I?" Aaliyah repeated as she spun around and around trying to catch a glimpse of her body.

"Pink," Liam replied.

"Fantastic, that's perfect," Aaliyah exclaimed "My favourite colour!"

Aaliyah waited patiently for her brothers to get used to the wiggle and flap and to accept the unbelievable sensation of being able to breathe and talk underwater. She watched as they swam about, gradually learning to enjoy the freedom of moving effortlessly through the water.

"Look at me," bubbled Hudson with his yellow and orange glow as he darted in and out of a bush of seaweed. Aaliyah smiled to herself. She was so happy and relieved that her brothers were here with her and watching them figure everything out was the best!

"So," Matthew bubbled feeling a bit calmer and starting to accept the shock of becoming a fish! "What do we do now? And can I just check that you know how to get out of here and back to normal?" He was working hard, practising holding himself in place with a wiggle and a flap, fighting against the tide.

"We know," Liam and Aaliyah bubbled together "Don't worry, it's quite easy."

"I'll show you when we are ready to go." Aaliyah reassured him.

"I suppose we could explore the sea," Liam suggested and the four of them turned and looked into the deep dark ocean that stretched ahead of them like a black thundercloud in the sky.

"Umm, maybe we should just stick to the shoreline for today!!?" Matthew replied. The three of them agreed enthusiastically. Each of them felt a little daunted by the idea of heading out into the depths of the ocean. They were only little fish and that was an endless pool of dark water.

"Great idea," Aaliyah bubbled, "Come on, let's go and explore."

They swam and they darted, they soared through the water as though they had wings, they held their watery breath and shot up over the cresting waves. They explored every part of the shoreline with Matthew occasionally checking that they could still see their beach and Nanny sitting patiently on the picnic blanket in the sunshine, probably daydreaming about her own adventures from years gone by.

Matthew kept a watchful eye that his brothers and sister were safe and staying together, he did not want to lose them out to sea.

"Oh my gosh I'm tired," Aaliyah was the first to admit.

"Me too," bubbled Hudson. "I'd really like something to eat," Liam mouthed loving watching the bubbles erupt into the sea around him, whenever he spoke.

"Shall we go back to Nanny?" Matthew suggested. "Yeah, cool," Hudson replied, "but will we be able to come back?" Hudson was really enjoying flitting about and showing off his new water skills "If this is only a one-time deal then I'm staying here forever."

"This is my third time," Aaliyah bubbled, "I don't know how many times we can go back and forth or what the rules are but I've done this three times so far so I'm hoping that we will be able to keep coming back."

"Ok let's go for now then, shall we?" Liam bubbled.

"How do we do it?" Matthew asked.

Aaliyah was secretly enjoying being the one with all the answers and she bubbled,

"All you have to do is wish to be back to normal, repeat it at least three times and wish with all your might."

"Liam can you show them?" she asked.

Liam swam in front of them and bubbled "Watch me."

"I wish I was back to normal, I wish I was back to normal, I wish I was back to normal" and !**POOF**! with a glimmering glow Liam was sitting in the shallow water, where he had just been swimming as a fish, but completely back to his usual self, wiggling his toes in the water.

He looked like a giant to the rest of the children, who swam around him gleefully.

"Stop it, you're tickling my toes!" Liam hollered as Hudson swam a little too close to his giant feet. They all laughed and one by one they wished with all their might and !**POOF**! They were back to themselves again, sitting in the shallow water like nothing had happened.

The four of them sprinted back to Nanny who listened patiently to lots of glwp, glop, glips while the children tried, unsuccessfully, to tell their story.

CHAPTER 7

GIANTS

That evening, after spending the rest of the day pointlessly trying to tell Nanny their adventures and only managing to make nonsensical noises, the four children were feeling quite exhilarated but exhausted. They were all cuddled up in their made-up beds, still excitedly chatting away, wording everything carefully to avoid making the strange noises even though those noises were really funny... "glwp, gurgle, plip," Liam said on purpose trying to say I touched the magic rock and giggling at the strange noises he was making.

"I wonder if we could write it down?" Liam said, wondering why they hadn't already thought of it. "No, we can't," Matthew replied "I've tried!"

"Huh," said Hudson "When did you try?"

"I tried on this," Matthew said, holding up his phone, "I tried to message Leo, Matt and Noah on our group chat but all the letters just kept scrambling up." He said sadly. Leo, Matt and Noah were Matthew's best friends, they were all in school together and they had been as thick as thieves since junior school.

"Oh no," said Liam miserably "I'm guessing that means I can't tell Max either?" Max was Liam's best friend and he happened to be Leo's younger brother so Max and Liam had known each other all their lives and shared everything in and outside of school, it would be so hard to not at least try to tell Max, but could you imagine explaining all the glurp, bloop, blips? Liam thought sadly.

The four of them sat quietly for a moment feeling very frustrated.

"So we really can't tell anyone?" Aaliyah eventually broke the silence.

"No, it doesn't look like it." Matthew replied. The thought subdued the children - all these amazing adventures and they couldn't tell a soul!

"I suppose," Hudson said quietly "We could show them." The thought of showing their friends filled the children with some hope,

"Ooh yes we could show them."

"That's a great idea."

"I doubt anyone would believe us so showing them would be perfect." They talked over each other.

Nanny's head popped around the door, "Have you all brushed your teeth?" she asked. "Yes Nanny" they replied simultaneously.

"Well done," Nanny smiled at them, "Get some sleep tomorrow is another day."

"Night, night Nanny," they shouted as Nanny blew a kiss in each of their directions.

"Sweet dreams my darlings," Nanny replied.

Aaliyah cuddled in deeper into her sleeping bag and could feel herself drifting off to sleep dreaming of bringing her friends to the beach and proudly showing off the glimmering rock. It was her discovery, after all.

All four children woke as soon as the early morning sunshine started to brighten the room.

"Come on, hurry, let's get going," they whispered eagerly to each other. Aaliyah could hear Nanny pottering in the kitchen and a delicious smell of homemade waffles hung in the air.

"Morning Nanny," she called. Nanny smiled cheerfully through the doorway. "Good morning, how did you all sleep?" She asked the four children but none of them answered, instead they all said as one

"Can we go, Nanny, can we go?"

"Hold on," Nanny replied smiling. "Let's have a bite of breakfast first." Aaliyah wolfed down huge mouthfuls of delicious waffles, she was normally a slow eater, savouring every bite, but this morning she was just in such a hurry to get to the sea. Would it be there again today? Oh, that feeling of swimming through the water, Aaliyah really couldn't wait! She gulped down a large mouthful of milk and with a milk moustache adorning her upper lip she gasped

"I'm ready!"

"No you are not," Nanny laughed and sent them all into the bathroom to wash their faces and clean their teeth.

Nanny was busy placing towels into a beach bag when Aaliyah came rushing out of the bathroom.

"Can we go now Nanny *please*?" She begged.

"Ok, ok," said Nanny. She had finished gathering everything they needed for the beach day and in no time at all they were heading off through the little gate enjoying the tinkle of the bell as they passed through.

The sun was already shining brightly and the early morning rays were quickly drying the damp grass on the pathway down to the beach. I'm so lucky, Aaliyah thought as she kicked off her flip-flops and ran onto the warm sand. Nanny's beach was amazing, the cliff up to Nanny's cottage rose high above them and she secretly thanked the world around her for creating such a perfect little beach for her and her brothers to play on. The beach was extremely hard to get to if you didn't live in the cottage right at the top of the cliff and Aaliyah knew how fortunate she was.

Very few people ever came to the beach as the journey down the cliff was a little treacherous if you didn't know it. Occasionally boats would come into the bay but there were some sharp rocky outcrops to navigate so only those who knew what they were doing would attempt it. That meant that Nanny's beach was mostly their own secret little seaside even in the height of the summer holidays.

"Come on Aaliyah!" Liam yelled already nearly at the shoreline. Aaliyah sprinted after her brothers and together they scanned the sea, frantically looking for the magic rock.

"It's there, it's there!" Matthew pointed, jumping up and down. A huge feeling of relief came over Aaliyah. It had moved since yesterday, but it was still there, a little deeper in the water but mesmerizingly beautiful with its glowing shimmering lights... Another day, another adventure. Fantastic!

The four children rushed into the water.

"I'm first, I'm first," her brothers yelled. Aaliyah waited patiently for each of them to touch the rock, then she reached out her hand and !**POOF**! The roller coaster moment and she was down in the sparkling water.

Oh, how she loved this feeling! She whooped and darted around feeling happy and free.

"Can we go a bit further?" Liam bubbled to Matthew, remembering that Nanny had said Matthew was in charge.

"I don't see why not," Matthew bubbled back, he was just as keen to explore further away as the rest of them, "but let's stay close to the shoreline," he said nervously looking out into the deep dark stretch of ocean.

"Yeah, good idea," Liam bubbled.

Together the four of them ventured around an extremely large jutting rock that separated Nanny's beach from the rest of the world. It was a huge cliff formation that pushed far out into the sea. It was rare for anyone to pass the point of jagged rocks but as fish, it was very easy for Aaliyah and her brothers. They swam around the edges of the massive rocky outcrop and soon drifted into the neighbouring beach, a beautiful stretch of golden sand that continued as far as the eye could see.

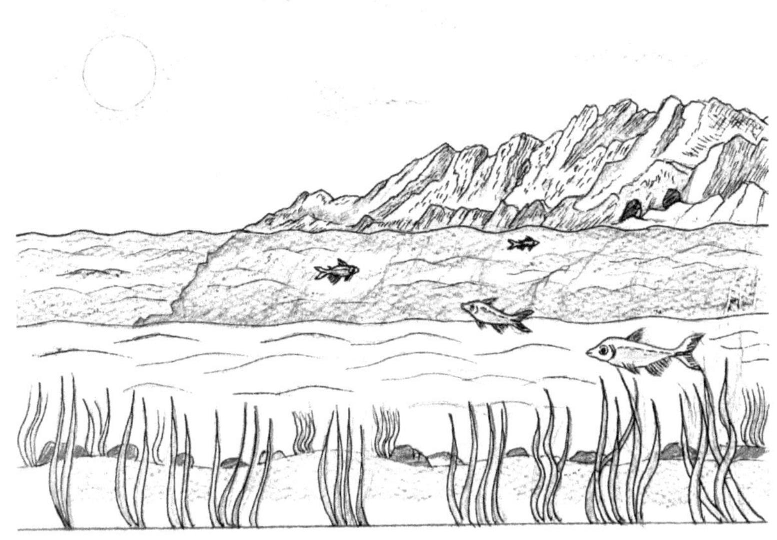

"Aaliyah, watch out!" Matthew let out a frantic stream of bubbles as a giant splash and something massive, solid and heavy pounded into the water throwing all four of them in different directions. Aaliyah was tossed high up into the sky on the crest of a large wave of water. She fell back into the sea, completely disorientated. She tried to get her bearings, to figure out what was happening but with loud noises echoing above her and something large that was moving rapidly, smashing into the water surrounding her, she was trapped and didn't know which direction to swim.

"Help, Help!" She bubbled, lost in the swell of the moving water. Aaliyah was struggling to keep herself upright as she tumbled out of control, in the sea. "Ow" she screamed as she felt something hard knocking against her. It felt almost like a branch of a tree was hitting her out of the way. Every time she managed to stabilise herself the tree branch would attack again, while she thrashed about, trying to get away.

Matthew suddenly appeared beside her.

"Aaliyah follow me," he bubbled.

Aaliyah was incredibly relieved to see her brother and followed him closely as he guided her through the water. Matthew cleverly navigated them safely under and over the smashing logs and as Aaliyah got a little distance away, where the water was calmer, she could see that it was massive arms and legs thrashing about in the water. A sea monster? What is that? They finally managed to swim back to the safety of the cliff edge and Aaliyah bubbled frantically at Matthew,

"What was that?" Aaliyah truly believed that she had been set upon by some giant sea creature.

"It's children, look!" Matthew bubbled feeling calmer now that they were safely in the shelter of the jagged rocks.

"Oh my goodness, I thought it was a Giant sea monster attacking me," Aaliyah said with a huge, long thin bubble sigh of relief as she watched a large group of children splash and play in the water.

"Thanks, Matthew," she bubbled.

"No problem," he replied brushing off her rescue as no big deal. Matthew really was a great big brother.

"Come on, let's go back to Nanny's beach," Liam suggested and Aaliyah thought that was a very good idea.

They swam carefully back around the massive rock and headed towards the shoreline of their beach. Aaliyah started to feel better when she was back in the safety of their little secluded seaside. She could even see Nanny in the distance if she held her watery breath and swam with super speed up, up, up, and through the surface of the sea, high into the air.

It took Aaliyah a little while to completely relax and begin to enjoy the afternoon again. Even though she knew that it had just been the arms and legs of children innocently playing in the sea she struggled to shake the awful sensation of being attacked and kept checking around her afraid that something was going to smash into her.

The boys quickly forgot about the giant children's attack and started playing happily in the waves. Watching Liam and Hudson race around patches of seaweed soon made Aaliyah let out huge ribbons of laughter bubbles and she began to feel better. She watched in admiration as Matthew taught himself to surf as a fish, catching a wave as it rushed to the shore. It really was very clever. It looked like so much fun that Aaliyah, forgetting her ordeal, decided to join in and was soon thoroughly enjoying 'fish surfing' as Matthew called it.

After hours of playing, tiredness eventually overtook the four children. Aaliyah had used lots of energy wiggling and flapping relentlessly so with some reluctance the children decided to head back to the cottage. What a day Aaliyah thought as she stood on Nanny's blanket and rubbed herself down with a dry towel. Being a fish is quite exhausting!

CHAPTER 8

THE TRANSFORMATION

"How many days have we got left Nanny?" Aaliyah asked. She had been awake for ages and was feeling refreshed after a great night's sleep.

"Well," said Nanny, "There is today then Thursday and Friday and you go home on Saturday morning."

Oh no, the week was passing way too fast! Aaliyah missed her Mum and Dad very much but what was going to happen to the magic rock after they had gone home?

Would it still be there when they came back to visit Nanny's next time? What if it disappeared out to sea never to be seen again? Nanny looked down at Aaliyah's concerned little face,

"Try not to worry sweetheart, just enjoy each day as it comes." She said gently.

Aaliyah and her brothers ate, washed and dressed as quickly as they could. They were very excited to get back into the sea.

"Shall we try going a little deeper today?" Aaliyah suggested feeling brave and strong.

"Ooh yes let's," replied Liam looking excitedly at Matthew.

"Ok," said Matthew "But just a little deeper," he warned, his instincts made him apprehensive about the dark water in the deep ocean. Matthew was nervous about taking his younger siblings out into the depths of the sea.

"I wish Nanny could come," he said suddenly, feeling instantly relieved at the thought of Nanny being by their side.

"Oh my gosh yes," said Aaliyah, "it would be amazing to have Nanny with us, I wonder what Nanny would look like as a fish." She giggled.

"Nanny," Aaliyah yelled into the kitchen. Nanny was busy clearing up and organising the picnic basket ready for the day ahead and had just finished putting apples in the basket. She looked up at Aaliyah.

"Yes darling?" she replied.

"Can you come with us? Can you come in the sea?" Nanny stopped what she was doing and looked at the children.

"I can't," she said looking genuinely sad. "I can no longer see the magic. I think when you become a grown-up like me the magic is harder to find." She said solemnly. All four children felt deflated to hear this. They knew that she couldn't explain it any clearer so they didn't question her any further, but they felt dismayed, it would have been so much fun and much safer with Nanny. Aaliyah got up and hugged Nanny tightly.

"It's ok sweetheart," Nanny said "It's just your turn, that's all, I have had my adventures." She smiled as her thoughts drifted off to her own memories. Then with a little shake of her head she picked up the basket, "Are we ready? Come on, let's go" and with a beaming smile Nanny hurried them out of the door.

Running through the tinkling gate and heading down the grassy path to the beach, Aaliyah started to get really excited again. I can do this! I can go deeper! I wonder what's out there? she thought. I hope we don't meet any sharks, she laughed to herself then quickly shook the thought from her mind. 'What if they did meet a shark?'

At the beach, the four children rushed around searching for the rock. It didn't take them long to find although it had shifted a little further out to sea, so they had to wade out deeper and dive under the water to touch it.

One by one they took turns to dive and touch the rock and with that familiar roller coaster feeling they were tiny little fish again, darting around, full of glee.

"Wheeee," Liam bubbled to Aaliyah as he shot past her using the swell of the sea to help him fly through the water. "This is the best feeling in the world!" Aaliyah let out a string of giggle bubbles. "Ok boys," she said bravely "Let's do this" and she turned to face the deep dark water ahead of her.

"Ok," bubbled Matthew "but let's stick together and if we have any problems we will swim as fast as we can back to Nanny's beach, agreed?" They all bubbled in agreement. Very slowly they started to make their way into the deeper water. Wiggle and flap, wiggle and flap, the movement which had once seemed so peculiar was now completely normal to them.

The blue water darkened slightly as they swam deeper and deeper, but Aaliyah was pleasantly surprised to find that far below the surface of the ocean was not as pitch black or as scary as she had imagined. Sunlight filtered through the water throwing flecks of gleaming light into the sea. The shimmering daylight gave Aaliyah and her brothers plenty of illumination to explore the large sandy areas and the grey craggy rocks of the seabed.

"This is fantastic!" Aaliyah bubbled to her brothers, "Look at me," she called, as she darted in and out of a small dark underwater cave that was covered in wavy green seagrass.

"This is unbelievable," Matthew replied examining an underwater snail as it moved slowly along the rocks.

"I didn't know we had snails under the sea?" Liam bubbled.

"I think it's called a whelk," Matthew bubbled back, showing off his knowledge.

"Look, look," Hudson yelled, bubbles popping all around him, "it's a live starfish!" They all rushed to watch the orange starfish move itself effortlessly along the seabed.

They were so engrossed in the water world surrounding them that they didn't notice a dark shadow moving slowly in their direction. It was only by chance that Hudson looked up just for a moment. Bubbles of complete panic poured from his mouth as he yelled,

"What is that?"

Matthew, Liam and Aaliyah looked in his direction, sensing the terror in Hudson's bubbles. "Oh my goodness, What is that?" Aaliyah screamed sending large bubbles in every direction.

A dark shadow was moving closer and closer towards them and was now very nearly right on top of them. The terrifying realisation that it was not a shadow shot through Aaliyah and her brothers, at the same time.

"Is it a seal? a dolphin? a giant fish?" Aaliyah whispered quietly as tiny little whisper-sized bubbles popped around her.

"I don't know what it is but it's heading straight for us!!" Liam's scream-size bubbles grew huge and then popped.

Panic filled them all and they darted around in the water not sure in which direction to swim.

"Head for Nanny's beach?" Matthew bubbled.

"Which way?" Liam bubbled back at him. Aaliyah's heart sank as she realised that with all their exploring, they had forgotten to pay attention to the way back. The ocean looked the same every way they turned. They flipped here and there, all the while trying to stick together but feeling completely lost so far below the surface of the water.

The massive shadow was now so close that it was towering over them and Aaliyah could see that it had its huge jaw wide open and was pulling in mouthfuls of water, filtering food straight down its throat. They were going to get sucked in!

"Swim! Swim!" they screamed at each other and they darted in every direction but no matter how hard or fast they tried to swim they didn't seem to be able to get away from the huge open mouth that was heading right towards them.

It was sucking them in!

"I wish I was bigger," Matthew bubbled desperately trying to find a solution to save his brothers and sister. "I WISH I WAS A PUFFER FISH, I WISH I WAS A PUFFER FISH, I WISH I WAS A PUFFER FISH!" He bubbled and wished with all his might.

Suddenly with a flash and a glowing shimmer, right in front of Aaliyah, a giant puffed-up fish appeared from nowhere.

Matthew could feel that something had changed, that he had transformed in some way, he felt so much bigger and so much stronger and he was very angry at the terrifying fish whose shadow hovered above them.

"How dare you try to eat my family!" he bubbled and saw massive bubbles form and pop as he shouted in the direction of the giant fish.

He swam towards the large fish with its massive open mouth.

"You stay away from us!" He bubbled so loudly and with such intensity that he surprised himself. The giant fish which didn't appear quite as large to Matthew now, took one quick look at the puffed-up angry fish and rapidly changed direction.

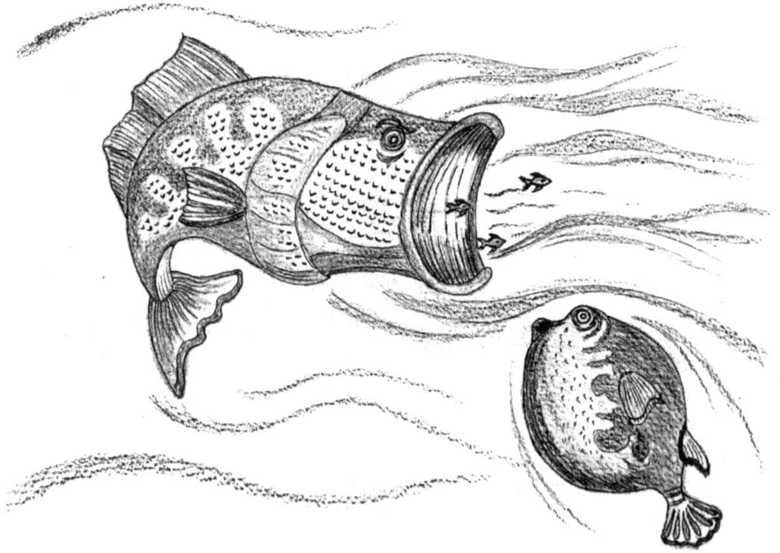

The children watched as the massive fish swam away, heading out into sea. Liam bubbled a dancing string of laughter bubbles as he darted around with excitement.

"How did you do that?" Aaliyah squeaked, bubbles of pure relief popping around her.

"Oh my gosh Matthew. YOU ARE A PUFFER FISH!" Hudson bubbled.

The three children swam around and around Matthew, laughing and bubbling with joy. He really was a puffer fish and boy had he puffed up, he looked huge in comparison to the rest of them. "Tell us how to do it please," Liam begged.

"I just wished three times with all my might," Matthew explained. Aaliyah, Hudson and Liam looked at each other and if fish could smile the three of them would have been grinning from ear to ear.

"I wish I was a swordfish, I wish I was a swordfish, I wish I was a swordfish," Liam bubbled without giving much thought as to what type of fish he could be. He wished with all his might and !**POOF**! Aaliyah watched as Liam glowed and changed right before her eyes. Suddenly a large swordfish was swimming happily around in front of her.

"Oh my goodness Liam you look amazing!" Aaliyah bubbled. Liam looked very impressed with himself and proudly swam around in large circles."

"I wish I was a dolphin, I wish I was a dolphin, I wish I was a dolphin," Aaliyah bubbled, wishing with every inch of her little body. She could feel the transformation, the sensation of being on a fast roller coaster and then Aaliyah was a dolphin, a beautiful, majestic dolphin. She giggled, a high-pitched dolphin giggle and WHOOSH she shot through the water, up, up, up she went and burst through the waves. She jumped and dived through the surface swell, bounding under, over and through the glorious waves. She felt magnificent!

Eventually she tired a little and dived back down to find her brothers with dolphin laughter still bubbling around her. She swam so easily and so gracefully. She glided back to where she had left her brothers and looking around she saw the puffer fish that was slowly looking less puffed up, a swordfish that was swimming around with its long, pointed snout and oh my goodness what is that?

A JELLY FISH?

"Hudson is that you?" she asked.

"Yes," came the reply from the wibbly, wobbly-looking jellyfish that was struggling to learn how to swim with tentacles.

"Don't touch him," Matthew bubbled "aren't jelly fish stingy?"

"Ooh, am I stingy?" Hudson bubbled and pushed a tentacle towards Matthew. "Argh" screeched Matthew as the tentacle touched him gently on his fin.

"Actually no," Matthew bubbled feeling annoyed at Hudson for touching him.

"Luckily for you, Hudson, that did not hurt!" Matthew bubbled as sternly as he could as a puffer fish.

The four of them swam and swam the ocean, floating high and low enjoying the rush of their newly transformed bodies. After what seemed like hours Matthew suggested that they had better find their way home.

Aaliyah bounced up high above the waves and there, far, far away in the distance she was certain that she could see Nanny's beach.

"It's there, it's there," she bubbled in her dolphin voice. It really was too far away to be absolutely certain, but they set off heading in the direction to what was hopefully Nanny's beach.

Aaliyah loved every second of being a dolphin and she looked around at her brothers swimming by her side. She started giggling strings of tiny bubbles as the thought occurred to her that they must be the strangest looking shoal of fish that anyone had ever seen!

As they approached the shoreline Aaliyah confirmed that they were at Nanny's beach. Matthew was relieved that they had made it back safely and suggested, that they had better turn back into small fish. "Could you imagine if anyone saw us, we would make news headline!" Matthew bubbled,

"A dolphin, a pufferfish, a swordfish and a jellyfish swimming this close to shore, we would be all over the internet."

They laughed, clouds of dancing bubbles surrounding them. It would be quite a sight for anyone to see. So, they wished with all their might and repeated three times I wish I was a little fish and !**POOF**! They were back, darting around, four little fish, tired and happy. What an adventure!

They coasted to the shore and made their final wish for the day.

"I wish to be back to normal, I wish to be back to normal, I wish to be back to normal" and !**POOF**!

They ran up the beach to Nanny, who was very pleased to see them. They had been gone for hours and had even missed their lunch.

"I'm starving," Liam said suddenly feeling ravenous.

"Have an apple for now sweetheart," Nanny said, "and we will head back to the cottage for a nice meal."

"Thanks, Nanny!" they chorused. "You're the best!"

CHAPTER 9

THE WASTED, STORMY DAY.

"Please Nanny, please!" Aaliyah could hear Liam begging, as she slowly opened her eyes.

"I can't sweetheart, I'm so sorry," she could hear Nanny saying. "It's just too dangerous in this storm, what if you get dragged out to sea?"

"We'll be fine Nanny, you know we are safe in the water, with everything that we can do." He worded his request carefully.

"I'm sorry Liam but I can't risk it," she heard Nanny say in a voice that allowed for no further discussion. Aaliyah jumped up and pulled the curtains open. To her dismay all she could see was heavy rain lashing at the window. The wind was blowing a gale around their little cottage and Aaliyah's heart sank, they could not go to the beach and they only had two days left! Aaliyah sat staring out of the window watching the wind blow the trees in the garden until they were nearly doubled over while the rain hit the windows in gushing blows. Aaliyah could hear thunder rumble in the distance. All the children were desperately hoping that it would clear up very soon. Maybe they could still head to the beach for the afternoon if the wretched storm would just pass by quickly.

"I've got an idea," Liam shouted over a clap of thunder. "Why don't we look up sea creatures, you know fish or sharks even," his eyes glowed at the thought.

"That's a great idea," Matthew replied, "maybe it will give us ideas for later."

Aaliyah understood that her brothers were wondering what else they could transform into. "That's the best idea." She said happily.

They hurried to grab their iPads and Matthew's phone and started researching different types of sea life. Liam was very interested in sharks and whales,

"Did you know an orca can reach up to almost 10 meters in length and weigh up to 10 tonnes?" he said gleefully. You could see his imagination running away with him at the thought of transforming into a ginormous whale.

Aaliyah was more interested in finding out about dolphins, it had felt so good to gracefully glide through the water. "I wonder what type I was?" Aaliyah muttered as she searched for 'dolphins' on her iPad.

"A pink one," Liam said.

"Really?" Aaliyah replied shocked. She hadn't realised that she still had a shimmering pink glow about her as a dolphin.

"I really liked being well, what I was," Matthew said cautiously and holding his breath he puffed his cheeks out as much as possible until he looked like a bloated hamster. Aaliyah, Hudson and Liam fell about laughing.

The morning passed slowly and even after a delicious lunch of Nanny's homemade vegetable soup followed by yummy fresh scones with jam and clotted cream, Aaliyah still did not feel better. She wanted to go into the sea so badly. Nanny glanced at the children's sad little faces and after examining the weather outside, she turned towards them and said "It does look like it's drying up a little, let's put on our coats and go to the cliff edge and see how choppy the water is looking. Shall we?"

"Yes please," they shouted. The four children rushed to put on their coats and ran cheerfully through Nanny's tinkling gate.

Standing on the cliff edge looking down at the high tide, Aaliyah couldn't help but agree with Nanny when she said,

"I'm sorry my darlings but it does look very rough out there."

The power of the waves crashing on the rocks was a sight to see. Their beautiful sandy beach was completely covered by the high tide. The spray flying up as the waves came smashing down was just magnificent to watch but looked very dangerous. Aaliyah could see that they could easily be thrown against the jagged rocks even as strong swimming fish.

"Nanny, I agree," Aaliyah said sadly, feeling quite afraid of the swell and imagining how it would feel to be thrown

against the rocks. It did not look welcoming at all, even as a fish, large or small. The children wandered slowly back to Nanny's cottage just as the rain started dropping heavy drops on their coats. The storm had not passed, what a terrible waste of a day.

Back at the cottage Hudson turned to Liam and asked,

"Can I borrow your iPad please, mine has run out of charge?"

"Sure," Liam replied kindly and turned to the box of Lego that Nanny had brought in for them all to play with. Matthew was already busy building an impressive looking robot. Aaliyah was contemplating going into Nanny's amazing sewing room to create something fun to play with, but she wasn't in the mood, she just kept daydreaming of being in the sea.

"Ooh look at this," Hudson said and started showing them pictures of what he called the coolest fish in the sea. Basking sharks, porpoises, stingrays, orcas. He was sitting on the settee enjoying imagining turning himself into a massive basking shark.

"Have you guys heard of a fish called the sunfish?" he asked them, "they eat jellyfish!" he said looking around him as if he was still a jellyfish and was about to be attacked. They all laughed, including Nanny who only half understood the joke, but Hudson's face was so comical she couldn't help but join in.

The day passed very slowly but eventually bedtime came and Aaliyah cuddled into her cozy sleeping bag. She hoped that tomorrow would be a better day and that they would be able to get back to the sea. Half-awake, half-asleep Aaliyah lay listening to her brothers chat about what they could be in the water and what adventures tomorrow might bring. "I wonder what it would be like to be a crab or a seahorse?" Liam was whispering as Aaliyah dozed off into a busy sleep dreaming of trying to stay afloat while the sea crashed all around her. Her dream improved when she turned into a dolphin, because then she found that she could easily manage the swell of the storm.

CHAPTER 10

THE LAST DAY

Aaliyah woke early the next morning and her heart felt like it skipped a beat when she saw the early morning sunlight shining through the gap in the curtains. "It's a sunny day," she yelled waking the three sleeping boys beside her.

"Huh?" Matthew muttered and rolled over, pulling his pillow over his head. Too early, way too early he thought and he lay there for a moment before the realisation that it was a sunny day dawned on him. He jumped up and bounced a little on his bed yelling,

"It's a sunny day!"

The four children rushed to pull the curtains back and looked gleefully out of the window at the glorious sunshine pouring into their lounge. It's a lovely day, they practically sang.

"Nanny," they shouted and ran into her bedroom "The sun is shining!"

Nanny smiled sleepily at them.

"Ok darlings I'll get up now." They rushed to help Nanny make a simple breakfast of homemade blackcurrant jam on toast and gulped down small glasses of orange juice. They hurried to dress and brush their teeth and in no time at all they were standing on the cliffs, staring down at the beach below.

"Let's do it!" Liam said and sprinted down the wet grassy path to the beach.

"Slow down," Nanny called after them, "don't fall." The treacherous path down the cliff was only dangerous if you didn't know it and the children expertly skipped along knowing exactly where to step and where not to step for fear of taking a tumble over the cliff edge. They rushed onto the beach and throwing their shorts and T-shirts into a messy pile, in their bathers they ran to the shoreline.

"Where is it?" they called out to each other,

"Can you see it?"

"I can't see it," Aaliyah sounded worried.

"Oh no has it gone?" Liam said. "Maybe the storm has swept it out to sea?"

Desperately, the four children searched and searched! With tears in her eyes, Aaliyah muttered sadly,

"I think it has gone."

"Oh no it hasn't!" Matthew exclaimed and pointed towards the other side of the beach and there in the distance they could see a glimmering shadow. The rock was lodged in the shallow part of a large rock pool. It was shimmering beautifully in the morning sunshine, glowing and beckoning the four children. They sprinted as fast as they could towards it. It was a good distance away from its usual spot, but it was still there! Oh, the relief!

"I'm going to be a killer whale." Liam said with delight as he raced to the rock.

The tide was still filling and emptying the rock pool where the magic rock had managed to wedge itself between two jagged points and Aaliyah knew that they had been very lucky.

If it hadn't gotten stuck in the rock pool, she was certain that the storm would have dragged their magic rock far out to sea.

The children stood still for a moment examining the rock that seemed to shimmer and shine even more magnificently because it was partly out of the water. The sunshine beaming down really made it look like the most beautiful rock that had ever existed. They watched in awe as it seemed to grow and shrink in size and all four were completely mesmerised. How did it do that? With a feeling of pure joy, they took it in turns to reach out their hands and !**POOF**!

Under the sea felt fantastic and they darted here and there, laughing and bubbling to each other "Let's go deeper, come on!" They swam confidently out to the hidden depths of the deep water and Liam was the first to bubble, "I wish I was an orca whale, I wish I was an orca whale, I wish I was an orca whale." And with a glimmering glow Aaliyah watched as Liam the  tiny fish turned into a humongous, phenomenal killer whale. He was massive, long and sleek, mainly black with white underneath and white patches by his eyes but somehow, he still had a red glow about him.

"Wow Liam," Aaliyah exclaimed.

"This is unbelievable," Liam saw massive bubbles escape his huge jaw as he spoke and he swam off - a glowing killer whale.

Aaliyah thought carefully to herself. She had wanted more than anything to be a dolphin again, but Liam's words last night kept popping into her mind.

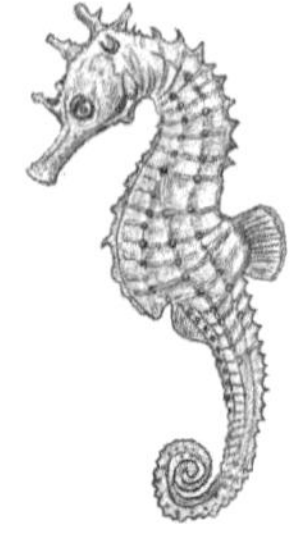

"I wish I was a seahorse, I wish I was a seahorse, I wish I was a seahorse," she bubbled and !**POOF**! Aaliyah was bobbing up and down with tiny little fins working hard to keep herself upright.

"I've got a tail," she bubbled in delight as she carefully figured out how to straighten and curl the little tail that had replaced her legs.

"I wish I was a crab, I wish I was a crab, I wish I was a crab," bubbled Matthew and a bright green glowing crab appeared in the water. He was floating unsteadily and slowly drifting down to the seabed below, but Matthew was thrilled.

"I'm a crab," he bubbled as he raised his pincers above his head and raced around on the rocks far below the sea.

He really did look hilarious.

"I'm a crab, I'm a crab," he kept repeating as he ran sideways under a rock.

Aaliyah turned to Hudson who had been watching his brothers and sister turn into the most unbelievable things and with a bubble of laughter he said,

"I wish I was a hammerhead shark, I wish I was a hammerhead shark, I wish I was a hammerhead shark," and sure enough with a colourful glimmer a terrifying looking hammerhead shark started swimming in the water above her.

Floating around Aaliyah figured out that her tail could be used to wrap around underwater plants to hold her in place and she sat there calmly enjoying the feeling of the motion of the water, the bounce of the swell of the sea and watching as her brothers explored every sea creature imaginable.

It didn't take long for Matthew to get bored of being a crab so next he wished to be a stingray and with his strong stingray fins he glided through the water exploring the rocks and sea life down in the depths of the ocean.

"This is brilliant!" he bubbled.

"I wish I was an octopus," Liam said excitedly "I wish I was an octopus, I wish I was an octopus" and !**POOF**! the strangest looking octopus appeared in the water, its tentacles thrashing around as Liam tried to work out how to swim with them.

"Ew these are so sticky," Liam said flailing his tentacles this way and that and then suddenly Oosh, Oosh, Oosh - the entire area was filled with black ink.

"Stop that!" Aaliyah bubbled as the black inky cloud floated towards her.

"That's disgusting!" She tried to swim away but swimming as a sea horse with small fins, progress was slow. Aaliyah remembered that mackerel are fast swimming fish and repeated three times.

"I wish I was a mackerel" and !**POOF**! She had changed and was swimming rapidly away from the black gunk.

The four children spent the rest of the day transforming into every sea creature that they could think of, from catfish to sharks and blobfish to sea turtles. Aaliyah's favourite, without a doubt, was being a dolphin although being a seahorse was a very close second. It was the most unbelievable day of their lives.

After hours and hours spent changing from one sea creature to another Aaliyah decided she wanted to be a dolphin one last time and quickly changed from her current manifestation of a starfish, which she had to admit felt a little weird, into a sleek and beautiful dolphin. She swam around gracefully and loving the feeling of jumping through the waves Aaliyah headed up into the last of the day's sunshine.

She surfed the swell of the sea, thoroughly enjoying herself until she became aware of how low the sun was getting. The evening was drawing in. She swooped back down into the depths, wondering what fish or sea creatures her brothers had turned into. Finding them easily she bubbled sadly,

"We had better go home."

"Why?" bubbled Liam. "I've only just turned into this Eel."

"I don't want to," said a very ugly looking Hudson blob fish, even though he had to admit that he was beginning to feel very tired.

"The sun is starting to set," Aaliyah bubbled, "Nanny will be worried."

"Yes," Matthew bubbled sternly "We promised that we would keep letting Nanny know that we are safe and we haven't… We'd better go back." They all agreed reluctantly.

"What shall we be for our last swim back to the shore?" Aaliyah bubbled.

"Ooh, good question," said Liam slithering past them. Being an Eel was brilliant. They thought hard for a second.

"I know, I know," bubbles of joy popped out of Aaliyah's dolphin mouth. "What about a Narwhal?"

"A Narwhal?" Liam bubbled. "Do you mean those big whales with the long pointed snout?"

"Yes, the unicorns of the sea." Aaliyah nodded.

"Are they even real?" Liam said picturing the animated drawings he had seen of Narwhal whales. "I'm not sure," Aaliyah replied. "Let's find out, shall we?"

"Ok," they all agreed.

Aaliyah wished with all her might and repeated,

"I wish I was a Narwhal," three times and !**POOF**! Aaliyah turned into a splendid looking mammal with a long tusk pointing straight out in front of her. She was a pink shimmering Narwhal.

"Oh my gosh, that's awesome!" Liam shouted and the three boys wished with all their might and with a colourful glow, three Narwhals, each shimmering a slightly different colour appeared. It really was a sight to see. They swam rapidly through the water heading in the direction of home. A school of Narwhals, with their shimmering glow swimming close together just below the surface of the water.

"I'm a unicorn," Aaliyah bubbled, delighted, as she raced her brothers home.

Back at the beach, Nanny watched as the four children appeared out of nowhere and came running up the sand to her. She had been a little concerned by the length of time that they had been away, but she welcomed them all with a huge hug.

"I'm glad you are all safe," she said. "Oh Nanny, we've had the most amazing day," they chattered away while they got dried and dressed.

The sun was slowly setting in the distance as Aaliyah stood at the edge of the sea. The waves ebbed and flowed by her feet and the warm breeze was drying her skin as she stood, sad that it was all over. She felt so lucky to have had such amazing adventures, but she was so afraid that after today, the rock would disappear and they might never see it again. They only had one more sleep at Nanny's, they were leaving to go home in the morning.

Please still be here when we come back, she wished with all her might staring directly at the magic rock. Please don't leave Nanny's beach, she pleaded. "Come on everyone," Nanny called and with heavy hearts the children turned and started the walk back to Nanny's cottage. Their adventure felt like it was over.

CHAPTER 11

HOME TIME

"Mummy, Daddy," Aaliyah yelled throwing herself at her parents. Even though it meant that their adventures were over, Aaliyah was still delighted to see her parents. She'd really missed them.

"How was your trip?" she asked them.

"It was good thanks sweetheart," Mum replied giving Aaliyah the biggest of all hugs.

"I've missed you all so much," she said lifting Liam into her arms. "So tell me what have you all been up to? Have you been good for Nanny?"

All four children smiled and giggled,

"Oh Mum, we have had the most unbelievable time." And forgetting herself Aaliyah said, "We found a glop grwp pleep."

Mum stopped and stared at Nanny.

"No way! It came back?" she said jumping up and down with excitement for her children.

"The bleep, plop, glwp," she said and the children all stared at her in shock.

"Mum you know?" Matthew asked.

"Oh yes, I know!" she said with a mischievous glint in her eye.

Dad was looking a little confused, he had only heard part of the conversation as he was distracted, giving his boys massive hugs.

"What's going on?" he asked. But no one answered.

"Come on everyone, let's get in the car and you can tell me all about it." Mum said happily, smiling at Dad.

"Ok," the children agreed. They felt blissfully happy again. Mum knew! That was the best news and although they all knew that they would have to word it carefully, they could try to explain some of their adventures to her.

As Dad loaded the boot of their car, Aaliyah ran through the tinkling gate heading to the cliff top.

"Can I say one last goodbye to the beach?" she pleaded with Mum and seeing her nod of agreement Aaliyah ran to the edge of the cliff and waved down at the beach.

"Please be here next time, please be here next time, please be here next time," she begged and wished with all her might. Hoping against hope that her final wish had been heard she turned and ran back to Daddy's car. She could hear her brothers still begging Nanny.

"Nanny can we stay just a few more days, pleeeaaase?" The boys stood at the gate pleading with Nanny.

"I'm so sorry boys, I've got things to do, I've got stuff to prepare." She said gently. "I've got to get us all ready!"

"Ready?" the boys repeated.

"Have you forgotten?" Nanny asked rolling her eyes comically. "Don't you remember? In just under two weeks, you are coming back to stay again," Nanny watched the smiles appear on her grandchildren's faces.

"And this time," she continued "your cousins from Ireland will be staying too, Aaron, Saoirse and Aoibhinn." They all whooped. Their cousins from Ireland! In all the excitement they had completely forgotten that their cousins were travelling over to stay at Nanny's cottage with them. Excitement bounced through them all.

"How many days until they come Nanny?"

"How many sleeps?"

"Just 10 sleeps," Nanny grinned at them all. "We are going to have some fun with everyone here together, aren't we?" Aaliyah couldn't believe that she had forgotten. In just 10 days their adventures would start all over again and this time they would have their cousins from Ireland with them. We can show them absolutely everything she thought picturing Aaron, Saoirse and Aoibhinn as little fish. To share this with her cousins will be the best adventure of all, Aaliyah thought happily.

⸻❈⟨❂⟩❈⸻

THE FINAL PAGE

This story is based on a real-life wonderful Nanny, who really does live in a beautiful cottage with white walls, brown window frames and a tinkling gate. The cottage really is high up on a cliff overlooking a beautiful, secluded beach on the Gower coast of South Wales.

The children are real, based on my wonderful children Matthew and Liam, who inspire me to write about amazing adventures. Aaliyah and Hudson are real, they are the brother and sister that we choose to have in our lives and are actually one of my best friend's grandchildren. Together the four of them create fantastic adventures.

The Irish cousins are real too and we are looking forward to their visit very much. Their names are genuine Irish names which can be a little tricky to pronounce if you are not from Ireland. They are pronounced - Aaron, Sir sha and A vienne.

In conclusion.

The cottage is real. The Nanny is real. The children are real. The beach is real. The cliffs are real. Whether the magic rock is real or not, well, I can't say, because you know I can't talk about it... glop, plip, glwp, pleep!

The End